This Little Tiger book belongs to:

_____

_____

_____

For Barnaby and Tina – M B

LITTLE TIGER PRESS
1 The Coda Centre, 189 Munster Road, London SW6 6AW
www.littletiger.co.uk

First published in Great Britain 2010
This edition published 2016

Text and illustrations copyright © Matt Buckingham 2010
Matt Buckingham has asserted his right to be identified
as the author and illustrator of this work
under the Copyright, Designs and Patents Act, 1988

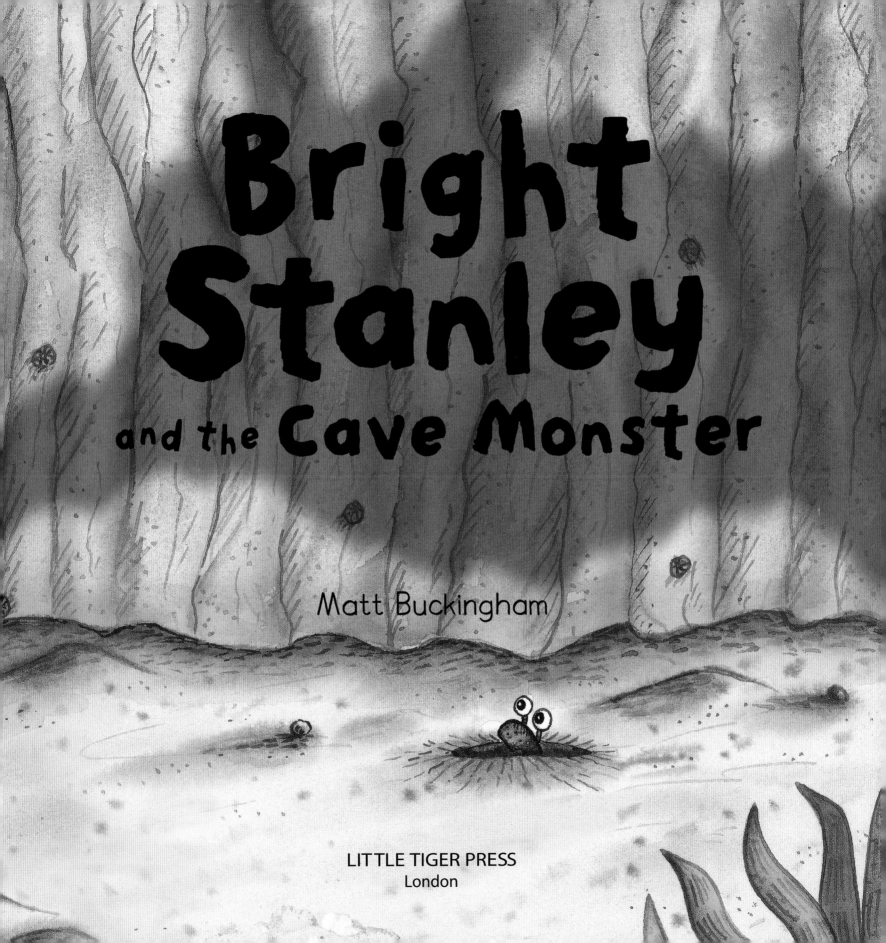

Bright
Stanley
and the Cave Monster

Matt Buckingham

LITTLE TIGER PRESS

London

Deep, deep at the bottom of the sea lived a sparkly little fish called Stanley. Stanley loved to explore. It was his favourite thing in the whole, wide world.

One day, as he swam happily along, Stanley spotted his friends, Percy, Turtle and Pufferfish. "Coo-ee!" he called. "It's me-ee!"

"What's going on?" said Stanley, swimming over.
    "We're going to explore this cave!" said Pufferfish, bursting with excitement.

"I'm going in first!" said Turtle.
"No, I am. I'm the bravest!"
said Percy, puffing out his chest.
"Oh, I love adventures!" said
Stanley. "Come on, let's go!"

Inside the cave, there were odd-looking plants and lots of strange, shadowy shapes.

"What a mysterious place," exclaimed Stanley.

"It's not scary at all!" boasted Percy,
swimming ahead. "See!"
But just then, he turned and saw . . .

"Hopping herrings!" shrieked Percy.
"It's a sea dragon come to
gobble us up!"

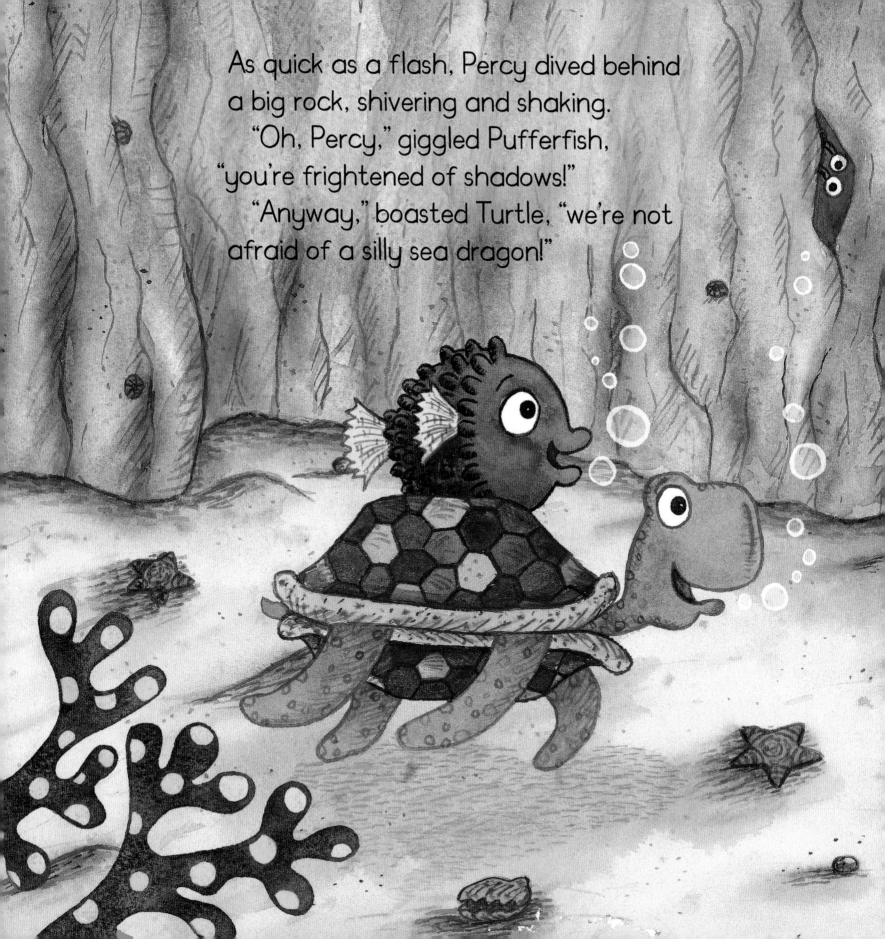

As quick as a flash, Percy dived behind
a big rock, shivering and shaking.
"Oh, Percy," giggled Pufferfish,
"you're frightened of shadows!"
"Anyway," boasted Turtle, "we're not
afraid of a silly sea dragon!"

"Don't worry, Percy," said Stanley.
"There's nothing to be scared of.
Just stick with me, you'll see!"

The four little friends swam on one by one. The cave was much darker now and everything seemed strangely quiet.

Out in front, Turtle and Pufferfish began to sing:
"Oh dragon, oh dragon, if you're there,
Come out of the dark, if you dare!"
But just then, right in front of them they saw . . .

. . . a **GIGANTIC,** wiggly tentacle!

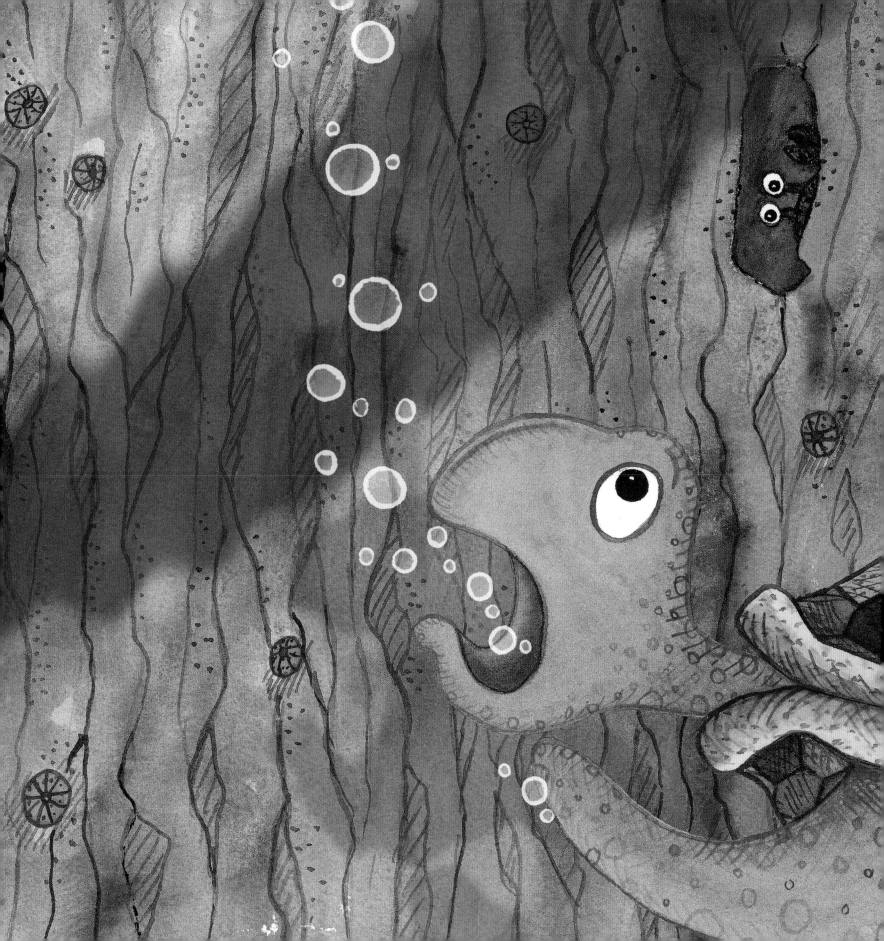

PUFF!

"It's a giant squid monster come to squish us!" squeaked Pufferfish, puffing up into a big ball.

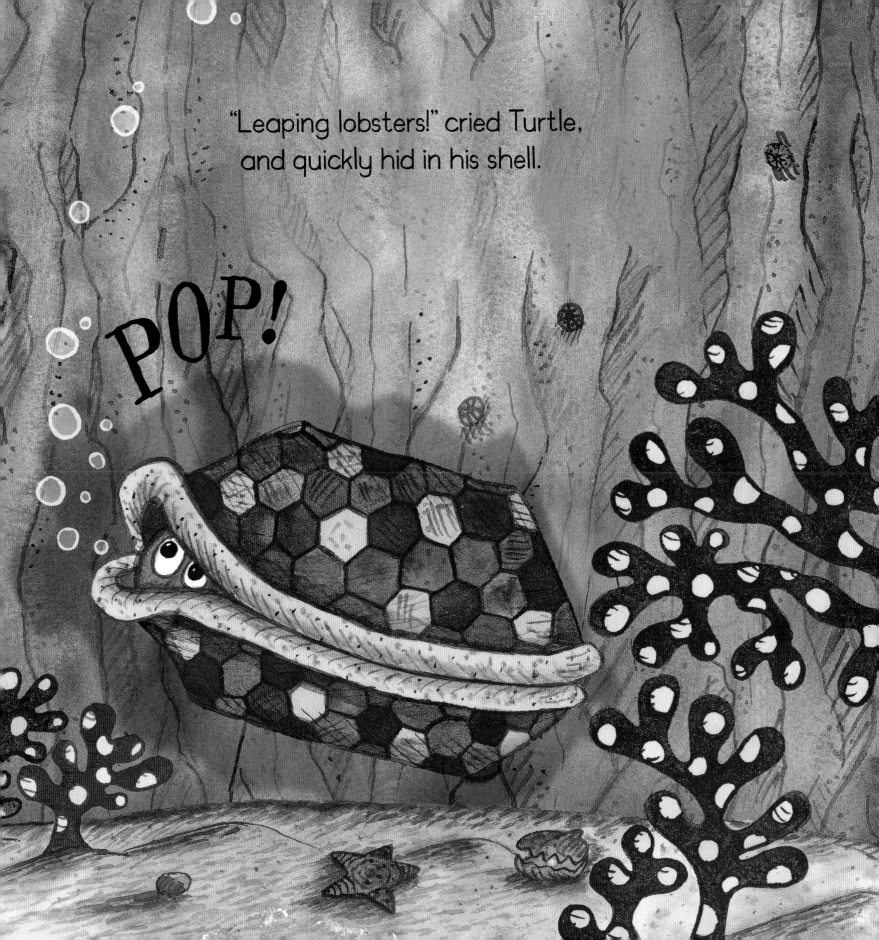

"Don't worry!" said Stanley. "There's nothing to be scared of. They're only shadows!"
"But Stanley," Turtle said timidly, "I think there really is a monster in here!"

Stanley smiled at his friends.
"No there isn't! Anyway, we
can't stop now – we're on
an adventure!"

Stanley bravely led the way.
"Coo-ee! It's me-ee, Stan-ley!"
he called with a smile. "We've come
to play, Mr Squid Sea Dragon!"
Then, from deep within the cave,
came a whispery reply!

The strange shadows got
closer and closer. Then suddenly,
in a whoosh of bubbles, out popped . . .

. . . lots of smiling, shimmering seahorses.
"You're not monsters!" giggled Turtle.
"We were frightened of your shadows!"
laughed Percy.
"Come on," smiled Stanley. "Let's all play!"

And as the new friends played amongst the sparkly bubbles they all agreed – this had been the best adventure ever!

More fabulous books from Little Tiger Press!

I'm Special, I'm Me!

Ann Meek
Sarah Massini

Bright Stanley and the Cave Monster

Matt Buckingham

MO's SMELLY JUMPER

DAVID BEDFORD ILLUSTRATED BY EDWARD EAVES

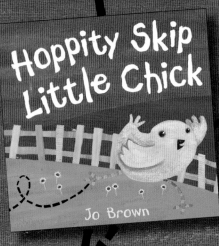

Hoppity Skip Little Chick

Jo Brown

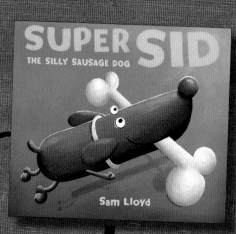

SUPER SID
THE SILLY SAUSAGE DOG

Sam Lloyd

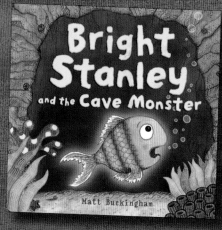

Joanne Partis
Hungry Harry

For information regarding any of the above titles
or for our catalogue, please contact us:
Little Tiger Press, 1 The Coda Centre,
189 Munster Road, London SW6 6AW
Tel: 020 7385 6333 • E-mail: contact@littletiger.co.uk
www.littletiger.co.uk

Image taken from *Hoppity Skip Little Chick* copyright © Jo Brown 2005